Andy and the Wild Worm

JANE THAYER Pseud.

Catherine Woolley

illustrated by BEATRICE DARWIN

William Morrow and Company

New York 1973

Woolley, Catherine.
  Andy and the wild worm.

  SUMMARY: Andy, pretending to be a worm, has
his mother guess what wild animal he is.
  [1. Worms — Fiction] I. Darwin, Beatrice,
illus. II. Title.
PZ7.W882Alg5   [E]   72-1981
ISBN 0-688-20061-3
ISBN 0-688-30061-8 (lib. bdg.)

ANDY was out in the garden one day, lying on his stomach and watching a worm. The worm was a shiny, pinkish brown color. It pulled its back end up to its front end as it moved along.

Then it wiggled itself into a knot.

Then it poked its way into the ground.

When Andy had watched the pinkish brown end of the pinkish brown worm disappear into the ground, he decided to play he was a worm. He went into the house, and said to Mother, "A wild animal is in this house."

Mother said, "Goodness, what
kind?"

Andy thought fooling her
would be fun, so he said, "You
have to guess."

"A bear?" asked Mother.

"No," said Andy.

"A lion?" asked Mother.
"No," said Andy.

"A tiger?" asked Mother.

"No!" said Andy.

"I can't imagine," Mother said. "I wonder if I could catch this animal if I put out some food."

"You might," said Andy.

"What kind of food shall I put out?" Mother wondered. "If he were a bear, I would catch him with honey. If he were a lion or a tiger, I would catch him with raw meat."

"But he's not," said Andy.

"Maybe he's an elephant," Mother said. "I'll put three pea-nuts on the table for an elephant, and I'll shut the door so he can't get out."

She put three peanuts on the
table, went into the other room,
and shut the door. Andy quickly
hid the peanuts behind his back.

Mother came back. "The pea-
nuts are gone!" she said. "Did
you see any elephant?"

Andy said, "He's not an elephant."

Mother said, "Well, perhaps he's a fox. I'll put a wee piece of chicken on the table." She put a wee piece of chicken on the table, went out, and shut the door.

She came back. "The chicken is gone!" said Mother. "But where is Mr. Fox?"

Andy said, "He's not a fox."

Mother said, "What can he be?
I know, a wild horse! I'll put a
lump of sugar on the table, and
I'll surely catch him." She put a
lump of sugar on the table, went
out, and shut the door.

She came back. "The sugar is gone," she said, very annoyed, "but I don't see a single wild horse around this place."

Andy said, "He's not a wild horse either."

"Oh, I'll bet he's a mouse," said Mother. "I'll put a cookie on the table." She put a cookie on the table, went out, and shut the door again.

She came back. "That cookie is gone, too!" she said. "Where is that mouse I was going to catch?"

Andy said, with his mouth full of cookie, "Hip nop a mowp," meaning, "He's not a mouse."

Mother said, "I don't know what other food to put out. I don't believe there's any wild animal here."

"I'll be right back," said Andy. He went out in the garden, dug up some dirt, and put it in his pail. He took the pail into the house.

"Why are you bringing a pail of dirt into my clean house?" demanded Mother.

Andy got down on the floor on his stomach. He pulled his legs up like a worm. He wiggled around like a worm. He almost put his nose in the pail of dirt. He said, "M-m-m-m-m."

"Is that the wild animal?"
Mother asked.

Andy nodded his head.

"A fish?" said Mother.
Andy shook his head.

"A turtle?" said Mother.
Andy shook his head.

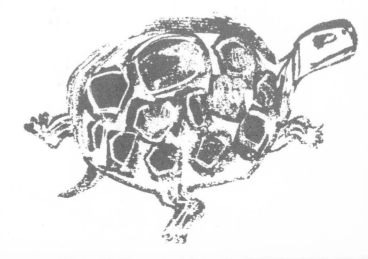

"A boy wiggling on his stomach?" said Mother.

Andy wiggled over and climbed on Mother's lap. He said, "M-m-m-m-m."

"What kind of language is that?" said Mother.

"M-m-m-m-m!"

"I can't guess. I give up!" said Mother at last.

"A *worm*!" cried Andy. "A wild worm! He eats dirt, and he's talking worm language!"

"Ooh!" cried Mother. "Get off my lap, you worm!"

"He's a nice worm," said Andy quickly.

"What color?" said Mother.

Andy couldn't describe the color of the worm so he looked down at his striped sun suit. "He's striped," he said.

"Does he have legs sticking out by any chance?" asked Mother.

Andy stuck out his legs.

"Feet all black on the bottom from going around barefoot?" asked Mother.

Andy showed her the soles of his feet, all black from going around barefoot.

"Why, that is my favorite worm! Where has he been?" Mother cried.

"Away," said Andy, "visiting his worm friends. Now he has to go away again. Good-bye."

"Good-bye, worm," said Mother, as Andy slid off her lap and picked up his pail. "We'll have some delicious dirt for dinner," she added.

Andy paused. He said, "*Some-times* he doesn't eat dirt."

Then away went Andy out to the garden again. Away went the wild worm to visit his worm friends.